R8 BY AUDI

A Crabtree Branches Book

Tracy Nelson Maurer

Crabtree Publishing
crabtreebooks.com

School-to-Home Support for Caregivers and Teachers

This high-interest book is designed to motivate striving students with engaging topics while building fluency, vocabulary, and an interest in reading. Here are a few questions and activities to help the reader build upon his or her comprehension skills.

Before Reading:

- *What do I think this book is about?*
- *What do I know about this topic?*
- *What do I want to learn about this topic?*
- *Why am I reading this book?*

During Reading:

- *I wonder why...*
- *I'm curious to know...*
- *How is this like something I already know?*
- *What have I learned so far?*

After Reading:

- *What was the author trying to teach me?*
- *What are some details?*
- *How did the photographs and captions help me understand more?*
- *Read the book again and look for the vocabulary words.*
- *What questions do I still have?*

Extension Activities:

- *What was your favorite part of the book? Write a paragraph on it.*
- *Draw a picture of your favorite thing you learned from the book.*

TABLE OF CONTENTS

EVERYDAY SUPERCAR

Audi's R8 delivers fast **acceleration** and driving excitement. It also handles busy traffic and quick trips to the coffee shop. With its powerful engine and brute style, it's the supercar for everyday driving. It does not have an everyday price tag, however.

The R8 guzzles premium gasoline. It might get a measly 13 miles (21 km) per gallon with city driving and 20 miles (32 km) per gallon on the highway.

In 2021, Audi offered four R8 options. A basic R8 uses rear-drive, meaning the rear wheels push the car forward. Some people think rear-drive handles more like a true sportscar. The R8 Performance models feature Audi's quattro drive system, which delivers power to all four wheels.

Audi released its first R8 rear-wheel series (RWS) in 2018. The company built only 999 of them then, and just 320 were sent to the U.S.

ESTIMATED STARTING PRICES

Coupé	$145,000	$198,000
Spyder (soft-top convertible)	$156,000	$210,000

The driver can raise and lower the R8 Spyder roof in about 20 seconds at the touch of a button, even driving up to 31 mph (50 km/h).

A RACING HEART

The heart of this street beast is a 5.2-liter V10 engine borrowed from the car's racing model. The motor pumps out 602 horsepower in the U.S. Horsepower measures the force on the parts that spin the wheels. An R8 can leave a long patch of tire rubber on the street with that engine.

Audi, a German carmaker, sells the R8 in Europe with a slightly more powerful engine than the American version. But the American R8 motor roars louder.

The R8 uses an aluminum **chassis** and outer shell. Aluminum weighs less than steel. A lighter car can reach higher speeds faster, because the engine doesn't have to work as hard to move it. The R8 weighs about 3,500 pounds (1,814 kg). That's hefty for a supercar.

The average American car weighs about 4,000 pounds (1,814 kg). It usually accelerates from 0 to 60 mph (97 km/h) in 7 to 9 seconds.

The R8 looks fast. It sounds furious. Twin **exhaust** pipes growl even before the car pulls onto the street. On the track, the R8 Performance coupe roars from 0 to 60 mph (97 km/h) in about 3 seconds. It tops out around 205 mph (330 km/h).

The Lamborghini Huracán supercar uses the same engine as the R8. Audi bought the famous Italian carmaker in 1998 for $110 million.

SLEEK SPEEDSTER

The R8 prowls the streets at only 49 inches (124 cm) tall. Many nine-year-olds are taller than that! The rear spoiler and deep sideblades add to its sleek look.

spoiler

sideblade

Audi Sport

The huge 20-inch (50-cm) wheels sit wide apart for better handling at high speeds or on winding roads—in warm weather. Supercar tires do not perform well in cold, snowy, or icy weather.

R8 Performance models come with tires made just for Audi. Look for the "AO" (Audio Only) stamp on the tires.

TECHY TOUCHES

The R8's deluxe cockpit shows off Audi's advanced technology. Drivers can customize the sharp digital display or connect with the world using the onboard Wi-Fi hotspot.

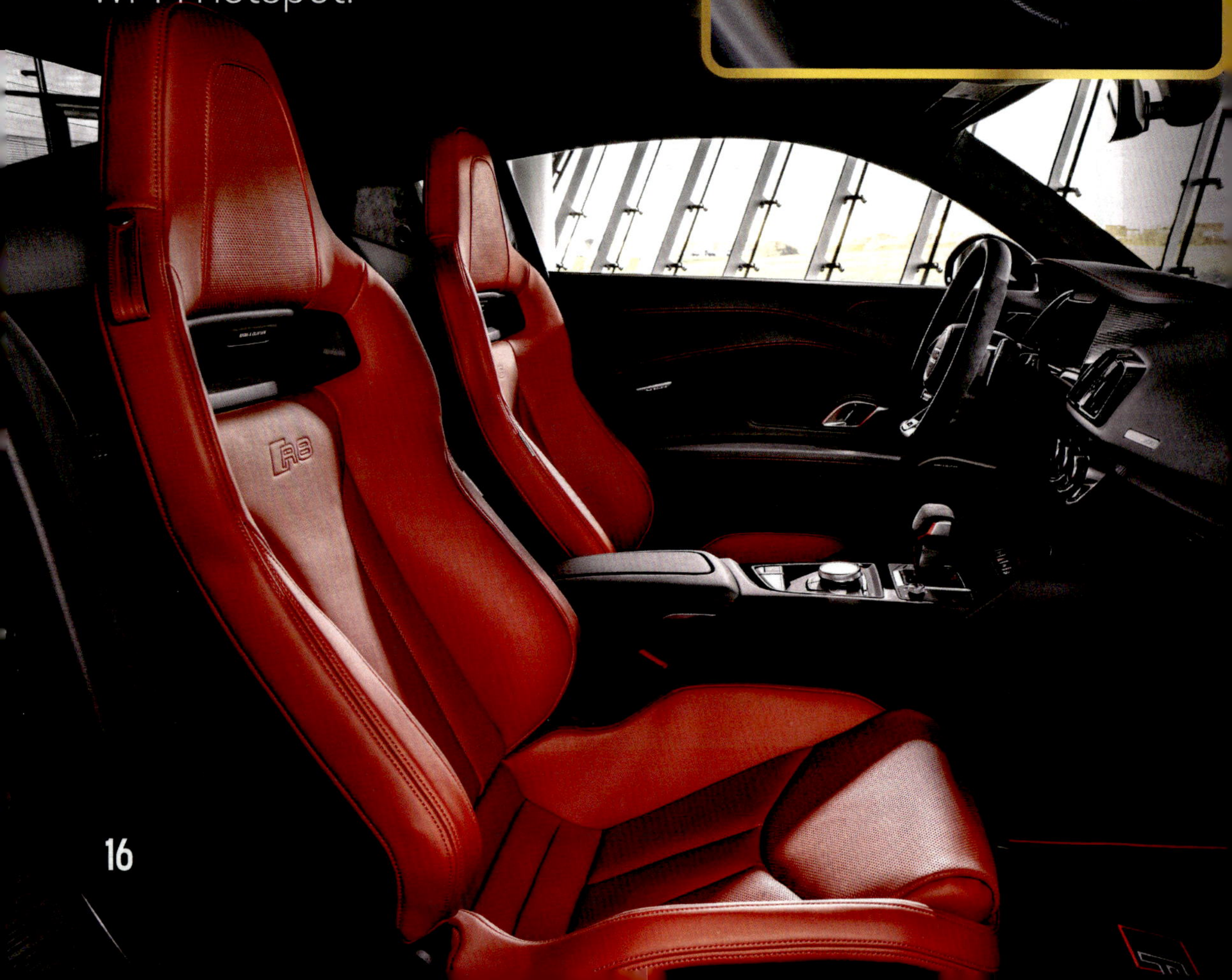

Check out the engine start-stop button on the steering wheel!

A luxury car needs a luxury interior. R8 owners choose black, gray, brown, or red fine Italian leather seats with a flat or a quilted pattern. They can even select the stitching color.

Every luxury car lacks *something*. For the R8, it's cargo space. Its little "trunk" holds one carry-on suitcase...maybe.

SEE AND BE SEEN

Bright **LED** headlights lead the R8 at night. A special laser beam also sweeps low and wide at speeds over 40 mph (64 km/h) to shed extra light on the road ahead.

LED taillights and **dynamic** turn signals that point toward the turning direction help other drivers pay attention.

Safety matters for any vehicle. The R8 uses brakes designed for stopping fast at high speeds. It also has airbags and parking sensors.

National safety agencies rarely test supercars like the R8, perhaps because of the small numbers of those vehicles in the U.S.

RACING ROOTS

Audi began its modern racing program in 1981. The company has won titles and fans around the world, especially for its **endurance** racing at Le Mans. The Audi R8 traces its roots to the 2003 Audi Le Mans quattro **concept car**.

The Type 42 launched at the Paris Auto Show in 2006, marking the first generation of the R8 road car.

Versions of the R8 race in major events around the world today. Look for this everyday supercar to keep turning heads at international races, private racetracks, and drive-thru lanes everywhere.

"Horch" means "listen" in German. "Audi" is the Latin translation.

The Audi logo has changed over time. In 1985, the company introduced the four rings to symbolize its four brands: Audi midsize and upscale cars, DKW motorcycles and small cars, Wanderer medium-size cars, and Horch top-class luxury cars.

EVERYDAY ELECTRIC?

The company founded in 1909 by August Horch has changed a lot over the years. Today, Audi builds most of its cars in an energy-smart factory on the Danube River. It's highly likely the R8 will become the everyday *electric* supercar in the future.

Both robots and people build R8s in the German factory.

The character Tony Stark drove a version of the R8 in six films from the Marvel Cinematic Universe, including all of the *Iron Man* movies.

GLOSSARY

acceleration (ak-SEL-uh-RAY-shun): To move or add speed quickly

chassis (CHAS-ee or SHAS-ee): The vehicle frame that holds the outer metal skin

concept car (KAHN-sept KAR): A working test design for a vehicle not in production

dynamic (dye-NAM-ik): Moving or a sense of movement

endurance (en-DOOR-uhns): Performing well and withstanding challenges for a long period of time

exhaust (ig-ZAWST): The waste gases from a vehicle's motor

LED (EL-EE-DEE): Stands for "light-emitting diode," a type of light source

INDEX

WEBSITES TO VISIT

https://www.audi.com/en/experience-audi/audi-sport/audi-racing-models/r8-lms-gt3.html

https://www.motortrend.com/cars/audi/r8/2020/2020-audi-r8-performance-supercar-review/

https://www.caranddriver.com/news/a34329012/2021-audi-r8-rear-wheel-drive/

https://www.caranddriver.com/audi/r8

https://www.audi.ca/ca/web/en/search-terms/LED-Tail-lights-Dynamic-Turn-Signals.html

ABOUT THE AUTHOR

Tracy Nelson Maurer

Tracy Nelson Maurer has written more than 100 nonfiction books for young readers. She lives in Minnesota where she happily drives a minivan.

Crabtree Publishing

crabtreebooks.com 800-387-7650

Produced by: Blue Door Education for Crabtree Publishing
Written by: Tracy Nelson Maurer
Designed by: Jennifer Dydyk
Edited by: Kelli Hicks
Proofreader: Janine Deschenes

Hardcover	978-1-4271-5485-9
Paperback	978-1-4271-5491-0
Ebook (pdf)	978-1-4271-5497-2
Epub	978-1-4271-5503-0
Read-along	978-1-4271-5509-2
Audio book	978-1-4271-5515-3

Printed in Canada/102023/CPC20231018

Published in Canada
Crabtree Publishing
616 Welland Avenue
St. Catharines, Ontario
L2M 5V6

Published in the United States
Crabtree Publishing
347 Fifth Avenue
Suite 1402-145
New York, NY 10016

Photographs: Cover: Logo graphic © Shutterstock.com/officeku, speedometer ©Cover: Logo graphic © Shutterstock.com/officeku, speedometer © Shutterstock.com/Panuwatccn, shiny car hood top left on cover and throughout book © Shutterstock.com/ Inked Pixels, R8 photo: © AUDI AG, title page: ©AUDI AG, PG 4: ©istock.com/Roman Stasiuk, PG 5: ©istock.com/DarthArt, PG 6-7: ©AUDI AG (all), PG 8: ©shutterstock.com/Levent Konuk, PG 9: ©AUDI AG, PG 10: ©AUDI AG, PG 11: © Jianhua Liang| Dreamstime.com (top), Domagoj Kovacic / Shutterstock.com, PG 12-13: ©AUDI AG (all), PG 14-15 ©AUDI AG (all), PG 16: ©AUDI AG, ©Domagoj Kovacic / Shutterstock.com, PG 17: ©AUDI AG, PG 18-19: ©AUDI AG (all), PG 20-21: ©AUDI AG (all), PG 22-23: ©AUDI AG (all), PG 24: © VanderWolfImages| Dreamstime.com, PG 25: ©AUDI AG, PG 26: ©Michele Morrone| Dreamstime.com, PG 27: ©©AUDI AG, PG 28-29: ©AUDI AG (all) Special Thanks to Audi.com for the use of their images to teach young readers about cars with nonfiction/editorial information

Library and Archives Canada Cataloguing in Publication

Title: R8 by Audi / Tracy Nelson Maurer.
Names: Maurer, Tracy Nelson, 1965- author.
Description: Series statement: Luxury rides |
"A Crabtree branches book". | Includes index. |
Includes bibliographical references and index.
Identifiers: Canadiana (print) 20210220589 |
Canadiana (ebook) 20210220597 |
ISBN 9781427154859 (hardcover) |
ISBN 9781427154910 (softcover) |
ISBN 9781427154972 (HTML) |
ISBN 9781427155030 (EPUB) |
ISBN 9781427155092 (read-along ebook)
Subjects: LCSH: Audi R8 automobile (Racing automobile)
—Juvenile literature.
Classification: LCC TL215.A825 M38 2022 | DDC j629.222/2—dc23

Library of Congress Cataloging-in-Publication Data

Names: Maurer, Tracy Nelson, 1965- author.
Title: R8 by Audi / Tracy Nelson Maurer.
Description: New York : Crabtree Publishing Company, [2022] |
Series: Luxury rides | "A Crabtree branches book." |
Includes bibliographical references and index.
Identifiers: LCCN 2021022142 (print) | LCCN 2021022143 (ebook) |
ISBN 9781427154859 (hardcover) |
ISBN 9781427154910 (paperback)|
ISBN 9781427154972 (ebook) |
ISBN 9781427155030 (epub) | ISBN 9781427155092
Subjects: LCSH: Audi R8 automobile (Racing automobile)--Juvenile literature.
Classification: LCC TL215.A825 M38 2022 (print) |
LCC TL215.A825 (ebook) | DDC 629.222/2--dc23
LC record available at https://lccn.loc.gov/2021022142
LC ebook record available at https://lccn.loc.gov/2021022143